V. Campbell

Alexander
and the Dragon

Alexander
and the Dragon

Story by Katharine Holabird   Illustrations by Helen Craig

Text copyright © 1988 Katharine Holabird
Illustrations copyright © 1988 Helen Craig

First published in Great Britain in 1988 by ABC

This edition first published in 1991 by softbacks
an imprint of ABC, All Books for Children,
a division of The All Children's Company Ltd
10 Museum Street, London WC1A 1JS

Printed and bound in China

British Library Cataloguing in Publication Data
Holabird, Katharine
Alexander and the dragon.
I. Title   II. Craig, Helen
823.914 [J]

ISBN 1-87504-000-7

For Adam
KH

For Sam, Tom, Jo and
Lucy with love
HC

Alexander was quite small, but he was very, very brave.
He wasn't afraid of dogs or thunderstorms; he liked
riding on roller coasters and swimming underwater.
The only thing that really frightened Alexander was the dark.

He always hated to be alone in his room at night-time.
His mother left his night-light on and read him stories
to cheer him up but as soon as she tucked him in
and went downstairs, Alexander began to imagine
all sorts of awful things.

He imagined that his door
was a mean giant,
and that his curtains
were two ugly witches,
and that his chest of drawers
was a fat old bear.

Then he would be very brave and leap out of his
bed and run all the way downstairs to his mother.
She would hug Alexander and take him upstairs
again and say, "Those are only shadows, darling.
Don't be afraid."
But as soon as his mother had left the room,
Alexander would hide under the covers and
put a pillow over his head.

One night at bed time Alexander noticed a dark
shadow sitting right under his bed.

"I don't like that shadow," he said to his mother.

"There's nothing there. Beds always have shadows and they can't hurt you. Now try to go to sleep," she said as she kissed him goodnight.

But when she was gone, Alexander was sure there was a dragon under his bed. He was so scared that he didn't dare move, and it took him a long time to fall asleep.

At breakfast the next morning, Alexander said, "There is a dragon under my bed so I can't sleep in my room anymore."

"Hmmm," said Alexander's father. "There are only two things you can do with a dragon. You've either got to scare it off or make friends with it."

And then Alexander's father went off to work.

That afternoon Alexander put
on his special helmet and
shield and found his
shining red sword at
the bottom of his
toy box. He tiptoed
up to his room, his
heart beating
loudly in his
chest. Whatever
happened, he
had decided
to be strong
and brave.

"DRAGON!" shouted Alexander loudly. "Come out of my room or I'll bash you!"

The dragon growled and its shadow lengthened
into a great green tail that slid from under the bed.

Alexander swung his red sword over his head
and bashed the bedpost until the dragon
snarled and flashed its yellow teeth.

Again and again Alexander
    charged at the hiding dragon,
        and finally managed to whack it hard on the nose.

"Ooh!" cried the dragon. "That hurts!"

Alexander stopped and peered under the bed.
The dragon's face was sad and frightened,
and he wasn't snarling at all.

"Come out from under my bed, please,"
said Alexander as he put down his sword.
"I promise I won't hurt you."

The dragon slowly crawled out and laid its head on Alexander's lap. "I didn't know that dragons could talk," said Alexander, scratching the dragon's ear.

"I didn't know that little boys could be so polite," said the dragon.

"At first I thought you were a shadow," Alexander told the dragon.

"Most dragons these days look like shadows when you first see them," explained the dragon, "and most people never can tell the difference."

"Will you stay and play with me?" asked Alexander.

So the dragon stayed in Alexander's room.
Sometimes it hid in the corner or under
the bed and looked just like a shadow.
Only when Alexander was alone did the
dragon come out and play with him.

"I made friends with the dragon under my bed and it's not scary at all," Alexander told his parents that evening.

"I thought he might be a friendly one," said Alexander's father.

"I'm very proud of you, Alexander," his mother said.

"The good thing is," added Alexander, "I'm not afraid of shadows anymore and I don't even need a night-light."

So after that,
Alexander slept
in the dark
and the friendly
dragon kept him
company.